Usborne Farmyard Tales

KITTEN'S DAY OUT

Heather Amery

Illustrated by Stephen Cartwright

Edited by Jenny Tyler
Language Consultant: Betty Root

Cover design by Joe Pedley

There is a little yellow duck to find on every page.

This is Apple Tree Farm.

This is Mrs. Boot, the farmer. She has two children, called Poppy and Sam, and a dog called Rusty.

Ted works on the farm.

He is helping Mr. Bran, the truck driver. Mr. Bran
has brought some sacks of food for the cows.

They say goodbye to Mr. Bran.

Mr. Bran waves as he drives his truck out of the farmyard. Ted and Poppy wave back.

"Where's my kitten?"

"Where's Fluff?" says Sam. They all look everywhere for Fluff. But they can't find her.

"Perhaps she jumped on the truck."

"Take my car and go after the truck, Ted," says Mrs. Boot. They jump in the car and drive off.

Ted stops the car at the crossroads.

"Which way did Mr. Bran go?" says Ted. "There's a truck," says Sam. "It's just going around the bend."

Ted drives down a steep hill.

"Look out Ted," says Poppy. There's a stream at the bottom. The car splashes into the water.

The car stops in the stream.

"Water in the engine," says Ted. "I'll have to push." "We'll never find the truck now," says Sam.

Ted looks inside the car.

He mops up all the water. Soon he gets the car to start again. They drive on to look for the truck.

There are lots of sheep on the road.

"The sheep came out of the field. Someone left the gate open," says Ted. "We must get them back."

Ted, Poppy and Sam round up the sheep.

They drive them back into the field. Ted shuts the gate. "Come on, we must hurry," says Sam.

"Stop, Ted, there's a truck."

"I'm sure that's Mr. Bran's truck in that farmyard,"
says Sam. Ted drives in to see.

"It's the wrong truck."

"Oh dear," says Poppy. "It's not Mr. Bran, and that's not Mr. Bran's truck."